WORLD WAR I TALES

TERRY DEARY

THE LAST FLIGHT

Illustrated by James de la Rue

BLOOMSBURY EDUCATION
AN IMPRINT OF BLOOMSBURY

LONDON OXFORD NEW YORK NEW DELHI SYDNEY

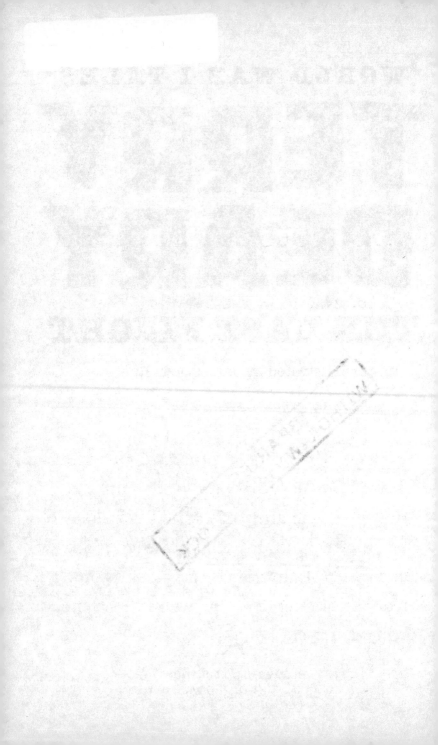

Chapter 1
Secrets and spies

Dear Lucy

Hello, little sister. I promised I'd write while I am away fighting for Britain. The trouble is, the army is worried there may be spies around. If I tell you where I am, and where I am going, then a spy could read this letter and be waiting for me when I arrive.

But I can tell you I am still in England and waiting to sail across the English Channel. You know I trained to fight in the trenches. Just before I left home we read the newspapers together. You cried as we read about the terrible battle at the Somme. Brave British men walking across the mud into the teeth of German machine guns. They were tangled in the barbed wire and thousands died or were wounded. You were terrified to think that could happen to me. 'I'll pray every night,' you promised.

Soldiers who came home from the war said they didn't do a lot of fighting. Most of the time it was just cold, wet and boring. Still, you were frightened. I can tell you, I was frightened too. I tried to put on a brave face for you, but I had nightmares. What would happen when the sergeant blew his whistle and told us to walk towards the

machine guns? Would my legs carry me over the smashed earth and the deep pools of slime? Or would I collapse with fear and have to be dragged by my mates?

But now I don't have to worry any more. And you can sleep well too. The most amazing thing has happened.

All the men were lined up to have their photographs taken by an old fellow. The pictures would be printed and sent home to our families.

Well, I know something about photography! Do you realise, I've been taking photographs since I left school six years ago, and I've had a studio for two whole years now?

I remember that last summer before the war started. The most beautiful summer of our lives. We went to Brighton beach and my photos of the swimmers in the glittering sea won prizes. You were so proud of me.

Well, as I was saying, this old bloke came along – and he had a pocket Kodak camera! Can you believe that? Even you have a better camera than that. I think Mrs Noah used a pocket Kodak on Noah's Ark.

He was shaking so much, poor fellow, he took forever to take one photo – and

there were a thousand men to get through.
So I said to the colonel that I had my Zeiss
camera with a Tessar lens. My pictures
would be quicker and much clearer.

The colonel didn't like it much because
it's a German camera, of course. But after
the old chap had fumbled around for ten
more minutes everyone was freezing.

'Here, Private Adams,' the colonel sighed.
'You take over.'

I'd finished in three hours. The old bloke
would still have been snapping till New

Year. And by that time the troops would all be in the trenches. But not me. That's really what I am writing to tell you about.

I am going to war but not in the trenches. It's amazing what happened. It was all because of my camera. I'd love to explain, but remember what I said about spies and secrets? I will have to ask the colonel if I can tell you what I am doing before I write anything else.

I have to start printing off the thousand pictures of the troops now. The colonel says I don't have to go marching on the parade ground – the most boring and tiring thing in the army. When I tell you about my new post you'll see why I may never have to march again. Ever. Hurrah!

Will you take a photo of Mum and Dad and send it to me when you reply? Just a small picture so I can carry it in my wallet when I have my great adventure – the one I can't tell you about just yet.

Love to you and the family, the dogs, and of course your dolls.

Your loving brother
Alfred

Chapter 2
Kitbag and kites

Somewhere in the East of England
Monday 18th December 1916

Dear Lucy

Thank you for your lovely letter, the photo and your prayers.

I've been moved 150 miles on the slowest troop trains in the world. The railways are crowded with men and machines being sent all over the country. We spent a horrible hour waiting in a tunnel while the engine steamed and tried to choke us.

It took me twelve hours to get here and I arrived in a darkened station around

midnight. The whole town is dark because of the blackout.

I stumbled around outside looking for a taxi and found one when I walked into it. It was a black taxi on a dark night. The driver was grumbling I'd scratched his paint with my kitbag. I was more worried about my camera in the bag.

He was still grumbling when he dropped me off at my new camp. This is the East of England. There are no hills to shelter us from the wind that roars down off the North Sea. The camp is as flat as the pond at the bottom of our garden and bald as Dad's head – not a tree to hide behind.

But I'm here now with a bed in a barn.

The north wind cuts through the planks and through my blankets. I think I'll wake up as a block of ice tomorrow morning.

Thanks for the Christmas present. I'll open it on Christmas Day, wherever I am. I have no idea where that will be.

My big news is that in future you must send your letters to Lieutenant Alfred Adams. Yes, I have been made an officer in record time! Only officers can do this new job and I am one of the best at it.

I bet you're amazed. I bet you're saying, 'What is our Alfred so good at? Is it his shooting?'

No, it's not. My shooting is so bad I'd have more chance of hitting my sergeant in the trenches than the Germans. (Hitting the sergeant is a nice idea. He never stopped shouting at me for six weeks at training camp.)

'Is it his marching?' you're asking.

No. Sergeant said I had two left feet.

Last guess. 'Is it because the men adore the handsome young warrior Alfred Terence Adams, and want him to be their leader?'

No. I will be an officer with no men to lead!

All right, I will stop teasing you now, little sister, and tell you. I have been made an officer for my photography. And I have been sent from the army to join the men in the kites. I am in the Royal Flying Corps.

Yes, I know I can't fly an aeroplane, but I don't have to. I will be what they call an observer. We sit in a two-seat plane. The pilot flies it while I lean over the side and take photos of the battles a thousand feet below.

It is an exciting sort of job, and a lot

safer than being down on the ground in the trenches. When you are in a trench you can't see what the enemy is doing. Is he

creeping round the side? Is he sending his big guns to a special place so he can blast our barbed wire away and break through? Is he building new railway lines that we need to smash with our big guns?

We can't see that from the trenches so we send up fliers in aeroplanes to take photographs.

Of course the Germans know how important those pictures are. They have special guns called anti-aircraft guns to shoot at the planes. We call anti-aircraft fire ack-ack or archie for short. You see? I am learning the new language of the airmen already.

But don't worry. The pilots who are training us say the ack-ack gunners are rotten shots, and so long as we stay higher than a thousand feet off the ground the machine guns in the trenches can't get us either.

There are also German fighter planes who want to shoot us down. I'm sure you've heard about Manfred von Richthofen, the Red Baron.

They say he has shot down fifteen British planes. But the sky over France is vast. There isn't much chance of running into him. And of course they will give me

a machine gun as well as a camera. So if that Red Baron comes within a mile of me, I'll shoot him down. (I know what you're thinking. I will have to practice my shooting if I want to hit anything smaller than Buckingham Palace.)

I still have a lot to learn.

Tomorrow I take my first trip in an aeroplane, over the fields of England. After six weeks of training I'll be sent over to France and join the war at long last.

Have a peaceful Christmas if I can't write to you before then.

Love

Alfred

Chapter 3
Flying and floss

Somewhere in France

Wednesday 3 January 1917

Dear Lucy

I have so much to tell you and so little time.

Your gift of woollen socks was perfect. You would not believe how cold the air is above the clouds. I hope you liked the leather gloves I sent you for Christmas.

21

We had goose for Christmas dinner, just like you! We officers get well fed. It's not at all like being a private.

Being a private all seems so long ago now. Flying may be cold but it is the most exciting thing I've ever done.

That first day of training in England was one I'll never forget. The commander told us we were needed desperately in France.

There is a big, big attack planned in the spring. (That's not a secret. But only the generals know where it will be.) We will be needed to take photos every day, three times a day.

Our lads have been sitting in trenches for more than two years. Now we are going to break through. The lines will change every minute and only the fliers can keep up with it.

First we were paired off – each observer with a pilot. I was given a young Scottish man as my pilot. You may think I am young to fight but he is just 18 years old.

His name is Donald Stewart and he's the nicest fellow I've ever met. He says, 'You're not bad, Alfred... for an Englishman.' Cheek. He is always smiling.

You will be pleased to hear he is also a great pilot.

After we were paired up, each pair was paired up again, with their machine. Donald and I were given a flying machine called an FE2b. I'll try to draw you a picture of it.

These are the planes we'll be flying now we are in France. You can see the propeller is at the back. What they call a 'pusher'. I get to sit in the front so I have a clear view to take my photos. I also have a machine gun to drive off any German fighters.

That part we sit in, the fuselage, is just wood and canvas, so it's cold once we rise above the clouds. The rest of the plane is wooden spars with wires to hold the bits together. It looks like a giant stick insect perched on the wheels of your doll's pram.

One day, when this war is over, you may get to fly. It is amazing.

Donald set off along the grassy field faster than Dad's Morris Cowley car. When we reached 45 miles an hour Donald pulled back on his control stick and we lifted into the air.

The clouds were slate grey and full of snow. But when Donald took us above them it was a sight like no other.

The sun shines down on the tops of the clouds. Remember that candyfloss you ate

at the seaside fair in 1913? Well, the clouds are like white candyfloss. Then when we came down below the clouds and I could see the patchwork of fields below, I could practise taking pictures.

Of course it's easy when there are no Germans firing archie or machine guns.

Now I am in France it will be a lot harder. But Donald is such a great pilot I know he'll always see us home safe.

Your flying brother,

Alfred

Chapter 4
Camels and clouds

Somewhere in France
21 January 1917

Dearest Lucy

I know I promised to write every week but I am so weary I can barely eat before I fall asleep. This is Sunday and my rest day.

Our training did not warn us it would be as bad as this. We set off each dawn with just a hard-boiled egg and a cup of tea for breakfast. Donald and I drag ourselves out of our beds. We don't speak much before we set off. He isn't quite so cheerful these days.

The FE2b planes are kept in a hangar and are warmer than us. Even in our sheepskin and leather, some of the fliers get frostbite

after an hour in the air. The trouble is, the FE2b engines won't start if they get too cold. Some of our mechanics wrap them in blankets overnight. There is even a story of a mechanic in the north of France who lit a fire under the engine to keep it warm. Guess what happened? The fuel in the plane exploded, the whole hangar caught alight and twelve precious flying machines were turned to scrap metal and ashes. One British mechanic had destroyed as many machines as the famous Red Baron.

Yesterday we took off at first light with three other FE2b planes. It wasn't like the training flights in England. We didn't climb above the brilliant white cotton-wool clouds – if we did that we wouldn't be able to take pictures.

And the earth below wasn't patchwork shades of green like England. It is a grey wilderness. No leafy trees or cosy houses or living animals. Only a shattered ocean of mud and shell-holes filled with icy water. Last year our armies invented a machine called the tank to crawl over the waste-land.

A few wrecked ones lie there like grey litter along with smashed guns. We can even see a few broken bits of planes, but we try not

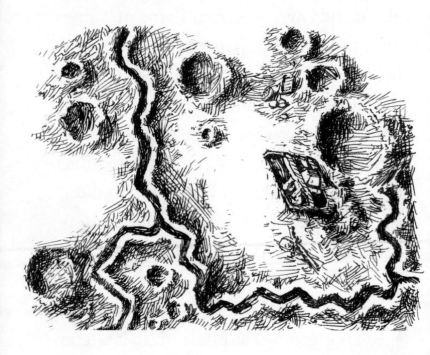

to think about them. A pilot like Donald will get us home safely every time.

I have learned that the FE2b is a very slow aeroplane and easy for fighters like the Red Baron to attack. Old pilots call the FE2b a 'Flying Bathtub' or a 'Dawdling Deathtrap'. But of course those pilots are still alive to insult the planes, so they can't be that deadly, can they?

We flew east towards the German trenches but we didn't cross them. When the cloud is low we have to fly even lower. The archie on the ground can reach us. Even enemy soldiers with rifles and machine guns can reach us.

That cloud can hide a thousand devils above us – German fighter aeroplanes with strange names like Halberstadt and Rumpler and Pfalz. But the most evil name of all is Spandau – the machine guns that they carry. When we hear the rattle and the chatter of a Spandau we head for home.

As I say, we didn't cross the battle lines at first. We had to meet up with a flight of British fighter planes, the ones called Sopwith Camels. Can you picture a camel trying to fly? Who thinks of these names?

The Camels fly above us and act like a shield against the German fighters to stop them diving down on us. Once our Camels are circling over our heads, Donald cries, 'Time to take our pictures. Say cheese, my German friends.'

Yesterday the German gunners were very good. I'd only taken a handful of pictures before there was a burst of archie just ahead of us. I could feel the warmth and smell the explosive. The splinters of metal ripped into the plane but I had ducked down behind my machine gun so I was safe.

Donald was supposed to fly straight ahead so I could get pictures five miles over the German lines but I felt him turn the FE2b towards the west. I twisted round and shouted over the roar of the engine, 'Where are we going, Donald?'

He pointed to his right. The canvas on the wing was torn and flapping and the wires cut through by archie.

The plane was wallowing like a whale. If we didn't get back there was the danger the Dawdling Deathtrap would fold like a piece of paper.

We headed home, and of course we landed safely. Donald had a grin on his face as wide as the Firth of Forth. (That's the river near his home town.)

'That was a close thing,' I said.

'Close enough but it will take a day to patch up the Bathtub. We get the rest of today off. Every cloud has a silver lining.'

Maybe it's as well that we did turn back. Maybe we are lucky. It seems the other three planes in our flight met a force of German fighters, the ones called Albatros.

None of our pals came home to base.

I hope they landed safely. But if they'd landed on our side of the lines they'd have been home for tea last night. They're

37

still not back. So they must have landed on the German side and been taken prisoner. Three pilots and three observers lost. We are losing them as fast as England can send them from the training camp. But not your brother, my dear.

I think the Germans look after the prisoners well. Of course, with Donald for my pilot I will never be taken prisoner.

I will have to hurry to catch the post now. This war will soon be over. Once we make that big attack in spring it will be over in no time. Make sure the kettle is on, Lucy. I'll be home before you know it.

Your weary brother,

Alfred

Chapter 5

Dawns and Deathtraps

France
Sunday 4 March 1917

Dearest Lucy

I hope the spring has arrived in England. I have been told I will get some leave and be home in April. Forgive me when I get home if I just manage to say 'Hello', and then sleep for a week.

The days are getting longer. That means

40

we get up even earlier and finish even later on the flights.

We are still losing airmen as fast as they send them out from England. They arrive one day and go on patrol, and they don't come back. So many come and go I can't even remember their names.

And so young. I'll be 21 on the first of June and I am an old man in number 48 squadron. Donald is still just 19 and he is now a flight leader. The last leader was wounded when his Bathtub crashed into a tree as it took off. Still, you mustn't worry about me. These young pilots only have about twelve hours' flying before they are sent out to France. They are like children driving a fast car, out of control.

But the longer you fly the better you get, and Donald is safe as the bricks in our house. I have told him about you

and he says to tell you, 'Lucy, you sound wonderful. Will you marry me when you are old enough?' I told him, 'She wouldn't marry a man who wears a kilt.'

I can spot a German fighter three miles away now – unless they fly between me and the sun. I know what to look for, and I can warn Donald and hurry for home.

Donald has learned that you never fly in a straight line for more than 20 seconds. He weaves around the sky like a Bathtub butterfly so he's hard to hit from the ground or from the air.

He can even fly the old Deathtrap like a fighter if he has to. We got a German Albatros on our tail the other day. When that happens you should never ever run for home. The German is quicker and he'll catch you, and you make a lovely target flying in a straight line.

I was twisting around with my machine gun when the Albatros attacked. But the German was a wise old bird and he dipped under our tail where I couldn't see him. Donald shouted, 'Hold on to your hat, Alfred.' Then he twisted the rudder and dived suddenly to the right. And just in time.

The German guns were rattling away – shooting at the place where we had been two seconds before. The Albatros roared past and climbed steeply. I knew he wanted to attack us from the front but I had the machine gun ready.

I had never seen an Albatros like it. It was painted red from nose to tail, except for the large black crosses on the wings. Lucy, it was the Red Baron, Manfred von Richthofen himself! And I realised, if I could shoot him down then I'd get enough medals to decorate your doll's house from chimney to garden.

I crouched. I waited for him to turn. I have never felt so much fear and excitement. But just as he began to make his attack he stopped and dived away suddenly towards the ground, with a Sopwith Camel on his tail. Our fighters had arrived to save the Red Baron from my deadly shooting.

They say the Baron has shot down more than twenty of our planes now. But he won't shoot down Alfred Terence Adams and Donald James Stewart. With my shooting and Donald's flying, we are just too good.

I have been told my leave starts on Saturday 7th of April. Five weeks and I'll be hugging my little sister. I will take the troop train to Calais, cross the English Channel, then take the train to London. I may have time to visit the shops and buy you a little something.

In your last letter you said the greatest present would be to see me come home safe. Don't worry. I will.

All my love
Alfred

Chapter 6
Biffs and Baron

Somewhere in Germany
1 June 1917

Dearest Lucy

Here I am, alive and well, but a prisoner in a German camp. I hope you got a message from the Red Cross to say I had been captured and that you have not been too worried. I am safer here than I was when I was in the fighting, and I'll be home as soon as we have won the war.

The German guards tell me the great British attack in spring was a failure. They seem like good men, with families back home. But of course they are sure they are winning this war.

You will want to know how I came here. I remember my last letter said I would never be captured. Well, I was. It was on 5 April and we set off at 11 am.

I told you about the Dawdling Deathtrap machines we flew? Well, now we have something much better. It is a two-seat plane called a Bristol Fighter, though all the airmen call them B-Fs or Biffs. It's even faster than an Albatros. Here's what it looks like:

Six Biffs set off that morning. I sat behind Donald in this machine so I could take pictures over the side and I had a Lewis machine gun to look after us.

The trouble is, they never gave us time to practise in the new machines. Six of us set off that morning, full of hope. Four would be shot down. It was a disaster.

It was a bumpy ride with a gusty wind and Donald was struggling to control all that speed and power. The old Bathtubs used to chug along together but these Biffs were all over the sky.

We hung around on the British side of the lines and found just four Camels to look after us. The big attack was coming any day now and there weren't enough Camels and pilots to shelter us. The Germans have a new way of fighting. They fly in a big group they call a 'Circus' – but Manfred von Richthofen is no clown. It was just our luck that we were flying in his part of the sky. And it was bad luck that the sun was shining that morning.

Donald gave the signal and we headed off to the German side to take our photos. We were too fast for archie in our new planes. By the time the shells exploded we were half a mile away. And then the archie stopped.

It stopped because the German gunners knew there were German planes in the sky. Before I could reach for my machine gun I saw a smoking Camel spin past us, shot down. Then the Red Baron's Circus was among us. They came out of the blinding sun, invisible till they were on our tails.

They were painted in a rainbow of colours. Swooping and shooting and climbing and tumbling and spitting lead bullets. 'Time to go home,' Donald cried. But he forgot the main rule of air war... don't turn and run.

'We'll be an easy target,' I called back.

'This Bristol is too fast for them,' he said.

He was nearly right. It was faster than an Albatros. But not when that Albatros was diving from high above us. We were still two miles from the British lines when the red plane swooped from the sun. I fired my machine gun but a bullet jammed in the barrel. We were helpless.

I could see the Red Baron's eyes behind the goggles as he aimed and fired. The bullets zipped over our heads before he roared past. But one had hit the engine and a blue-white flame appeared before the engine stopped.

We were drifting like a paper glider. The Red Baron turned in a circle and came on our tail again. 'Will we make it?' I asked as the wind whispered through the wires.

'Not if our red friend shoots us again. It's like shooting fish in a barrel,' Donald said.

I have to be honest, Lucy. I started to say my prayers. I thought of you and said goodbye to you in my mind.

Then an odd thing happened. The Red Baron sat on our tail and followed us down.

As we flew over the German lines the enemy soldiers opened fire with their rifles. We'd heard stories that Germans gave extra food to any soldier who killed a British airman.

Donald saw a flat stretch of road behind the German trenches. He brought us down and we bounced along and rolled to a stop.

As I got out, Donald jumped down from his seat and ran to the front. He drew his pistol and fired at the fuel tank till it split. Petrol poured out.

The German troops stopped firing and I heard the throb of an aeroplane engine. The Red Baron was landing behind us.

'We need to set fire to the plane,' Donald said and drew a box of matches from his pocket.

The German pilot had stopped but left his engine running. He drew a pistol and ran towards us. 'Stop!' he cried. 'Stop or I shoot you.'

Donald threw his pistol to the ground. 'You can't shoot a man without a gun,' he laughed, and pulled a match from the box.

Manfred von Richthofen pushed up his goggles. His ice-blue eyes turned on me. He shrugged and pointed his gun at me.

'Stop, or I shoot your friend. He has a gun.' I did. It was still in its leather pouch.

Donald threw down the box and the matches spilled in the road. He looked sour and defeated, but he had chosen to save my life. 'You're not bad, Donald,' I muttered. 'For a Scotsman.'

Von Richthofen strolled across. He had cropped fair hair and a gaze like steel. He bared his teeth in a cold smile and held out his hand to Donald. They shook hands. 'Welcome to Germany. You will be our guest until we have won this war.'

'Your guest till we win the war,' Donald said, his gaze as hard as the Red Baron's.

The Red Baron shook his head slowly, pointed his pistol at us and waved towards the trenches where a dozen German soldiers had a dozen German rifles pointed at us.

We walked towards our captors. 'He could have blown us out of the sky,' I muttered. 'Why didn't he? Is he such a good sport?'

Donald laughed bitterly. 'No, Alfred, it's the new Bristol plane. The Germans want to capture a Bristol in one piece and see what makes it so good. They have it now.'

'And us?'

'The war is over for us,' Donald said with a sigh.

And so it is, Lucy. I am in the German prison camp now. The Red Cross will carry our letters. But I am safer than I have ever been, except for the terrible food. The Germans are short of food. It isn't guns and planes that will win this war, Lucy. It is hunger.

I'm 21 today. I hope Donald and I get to spend my 22nd birthday with you. Keep praying for me. I'm sure it works!

Love

Alfred

Did you know?

The Great War was the first war to see aircraft used. At first they would fly over enemy armies and photograph their positions or to bomb them. Then the defenders sent fighters to shoot down these spy planes. War in the air had begun.

Photographer Alfred Adams was born on 1 June 1896 and became an observer in WWI, taking pictures over enemy lines. He was shot down by the famous 'Red Baron' Manfred von Richthofen over France, along with his pilot Donald Stewart, on 5 April 1917. They landed across enemy lines and both survived as prisoners of war.

The big Spring attack started four days later on the snowy morning of 9 April. Two and a half million massive shells smashed into the German trenches in that one week near

Alfred's airfield – but the British failed to break through. The war went on another year and a half.

The Bristol Fighters began to fly that month but on that 5 April day a patrol of six planes from 48 Squadron had four of their new planes shot down by Baron Richtofen's Circus. Alfred Adams and Donald Stewart were one of the four crews and they landed on German soil. They were the Red Baron's 36th victims.

Manfred von Richtofen went on to shoot down 80 enemy planes before he was brought down by the bullet from a soldier on the ground, a year after Adams and Stewart were captured.

The Red Baron never lived to see Germany lose the war in November 1918.

What next?

1.   Prisoners of war were usually kept in a camp. The camp would have huts for the prisoners to live in and sleep in. There would be a high wire fence around it with guards in towers along the fence. They would have spotlights at night, guns and maybe dogs. Draw a plan of a camp with 10 huts and then write a message to your friends in the camp. Tell them how you plan to escape.

2.   Prisoners were allowed to send letters home. The enemy would read the letters before they left the camp. If you wanted to send a secret message out then you had to use a secret code. Make up a code and send a message. See if a friend can read it.

3. Prisoners would also use invisible ink. A simple invisible ink is made with lemon juice. Try writing a message to a friend asking for something to help your escape plan – a set of wire clippers, a map of the way home or sleeping pills that will send the guard dogs snoring. If your friend warms the paper then the lemon writing will appear.

TERRY DEARY

Victorian Tales

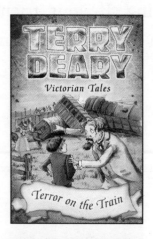

Terror on the Train

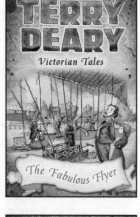

The Fabulous Flyer

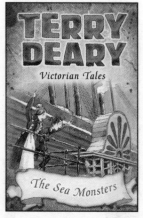

The Sea Monsters

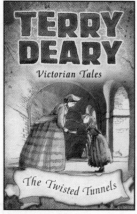

The Twisted Tunnels